I0631734

Scribbles

A pencil born without an eraser

written and illustrated by
André Hutchinson

Scribbles - A Pencil Born Without An Eraser
Copyright © 2020 by André Hutchinson

All rights reserved. No part of this book may be reproduced
or transmitted in any form or by any means without written
permission from the author.

ISBN 978-0-578-66599-3

Back in art school, we used to have this exercise called:
taking a line for a walk - where you'd put pencil to a piece of paper and
with that continuous line, you'd form an image whether intentionally or not.

Allow me to reintroduce you to a world of lines, marks, sketches,
jottings, shapes, images and stories. Stories from my own experiences and
imagination. Has anyone stopped and thought about the history of the
creativity companion? I know I have... To begin, lets first imagine what
happens when your parents leave their pencils behind at the office, when
you put your pencils away after school, when you finish a grueling exam
or when you simply get lost in thought... Tap tap...tap tap...

Tap into what these precious writing instruments get into when no one is
around. Tap into a world filled with possibilities and potential.

So I've written these stories with the voice of our wooded and graphite
companion which will also touch on every day and modern issues that
can find us when we are stuck and buffering on a project.

This is the first mark on paper...let me guide you as we take that walk...

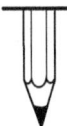

Prologue

Stories are told, fables spun and folklore lives on infamy.
But there are no tales for the motionless, and those considered inanimate
tools. Let me take you into a cup, a desk drawer, a stationery closet.
Let's mark out a tale of our favorite doodling tool...
A trusty number 2 pencil

Chapter 9B
Where did I put that pencil?

"**W**hoa!" - I whispered.
My eyes lit up with excitement.

'I can draw...I can draw..." But then I stopped myself.

Everyone can draw; some better than others, but the ability is there. We are pencils after all. We all live in the world of Marking Tools.

My name is Scribbles, but everyone calls me Scribs, and when I get into trouble at school my mom calls me: "Scribbles St. Mark! When I catch you, I'm going to strip the yellow off you..."

I love my Mom, but she smothers me a bit.... ok a lot.
I understand why, but I wish she'd give me more space. I know I'm a bit different from the other kids, but I'm not a baby anymore. I was born without an eraser.

Yellow like the rest of my number two family, but no ferrule for my fluffy pink rubber to grow into. I can write just fine, I had to practice harder than others and I hardly made any mistakes-unless it's something new. Then I just had to practice more. Moms always told me,

"Scribsy, you need to slow down, I don't want you to get any shorter from all that sharpening you have to do when you rub down your point!"

"But mom I hate staying back with the soft point kids, they leave smudge marks on everything!"

"Well it's either that or I keep you home and teach you myself."

"Ok moms, I already see you enough when you make me check in with you at the library every lunch time and break time..."

"Well you know I've got to work now since your..."

She saw my face...She stopped talking and went back to do whatever Librarians do.

My family... Jade aka Bubble Belly, Summer aka Loud Mouth/Yeller, Moms and...Pops

It's been two years now...Since he left for work and never came back home. I'm not sure if I should have seen this coming, but... I've felt the distance growing, like when you lay on a raft staring up at the stars, not realizing you'd drifted too far from the shore...then no one comes looking for you.

Well... At least that's how I heard Moms explaining it one day to the neighbors.

What about me? What do I think happened?
I just think Pops is working on a top-secret job, and they won't let him leave until it's done. What I did see though, was Pops being secretive with some old crumpled up blue plans. Only working on it when everyone was sleeping...well almost everyone.

Whack!

"Who are you calling Bubble Belly?" Jade bellowed.

"Why are you always spying on me Bubble...."

Whack again...

"Jade, will you stop hitting me...dang!"

"I'll tell mom you down here rubbing you point down and being mean to your little sister."

"I'll have you know this is homework, to draw my family and the monster that ate them, along with everything else....Bubble Belly"

Whack!

"I heard that!" As she stormed upstairs.

So that's my sister, well one of them.

I'm in the middle of a gross girl sandwich, where the older top bread Jade aka Bubble Belly, is soggy, from eating everything in sight and the other younger bread Summer aka Yeller never shuts up.

Which is quite common for a 2-year-old, or so I've been told by the giant source of random information. No, no, no. Not trivia, just random info that no one asked for I might add. And no one, I mean no-one can stop the source...I call it the Charc Report.

That's my neighbor Charcolé, I think she's a grown-up version of my baby sister Summer, but not as needy and not as loud.

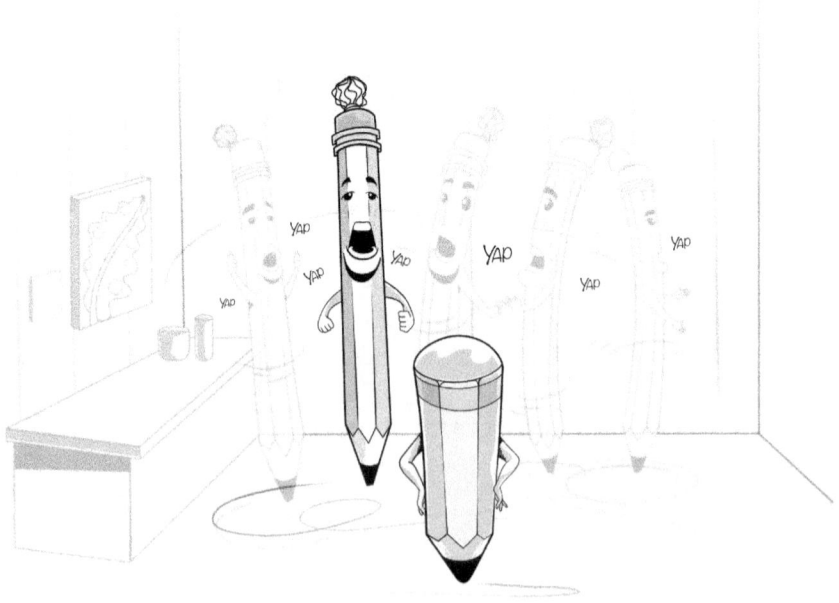

She must have traded all that loud neediness in for the "running of the mouth disease".

At times she'd come over all animated and attack my ears with the Charc Report, back when we just realized Pops was gone for too long this time. Moms would get really overly protective and I wasn't allowed to go to school with the other 9yr olds, Jade got put on a stricter curfew, which she'd break every now and then, then got chewed out, after that no one was allowed to leave the house. No daycare for Summer, no trips to the sharpening station for me...well for everyone,

Moms had some books and work sent home from the library and we'd all sit in a room to "study". This took place in the drawing room or kitchen depending on how much Summer would yell for food. She was a better teacher anyways, she always boasted.

And if I wanted to play, I had my sisters to play with. Which always ended up with me in the basement after I'd pinch Summer's eraser and she'd live up to her nickname "Yell-High" or I'd mumbled something "lippy" under my breath and Jade would "bite my head off".

This would go on for at least a week or two weeks at a time. So as much as she was annoying, she was my source of knowledge when I was being home schooled. I did learn a couple of things from her, like the Magician and the "Shinys" right across from the prep school.

"So…there was this huge ladder on the ground… big bold & white, that stretches across the long winding river of the Shinys, and then the Shinys came in different colors and would roar along within the borders of the dark river at various speeds, and then the Magician of the white ladder would make all the Shinys stop by waving an octagon wand with big white letters, with a special incantation on it and then the magician would wave to the kids and they would hurry across the ladder safely to the other side, and then he'd wave his wand again and the Shinys would make a loud growl & speed off again. Sometimes if it's dark enough from the puffy marshmellows of the sky or the tiredness of the sun, you would see the trails of red beams as the Shinys fade away into the distance, and then…and then…"

At nights, I got up and snuck down to the musty, sometimes chilly and dark basement, the desk lamp light would be the only light source. I usually zoned out for a while, and I would spin her stories. After, I'd find myself in the basement, just sketching away, imagining how everything looked, spinning Charcs' details in my head and being pushed and pulled in different directions. Sometimes with very jittery, up and down in long gliding strokes, I'd lean from side to side, standing up right when making sharper strokes, I was like an ice-skating water bender. Other times it would be deliberate markings, mundane continuous strokes, I'd do this for awhile, then I'd snap out of it, like a trance and see the pattern that was formed.

For hours it would just be me and the papers. I wasn't brave enough for the canvasses Pops had all over the basement...I always liked it down there...alone or with Pops. I crept down to the basement to practice perfecting my lines, so that it wouldn't be obvious that I can't erase them and start over at school. Then by accident or something, I'm not sure how it happened or what I was thinking...but there it was.

I may have gone for at least 15mins in before I realized. That was also the first time I felt something else in the room with me ...and someone was missing.

"Oh Pops..."

I remembered how Pops used to take me out with him on some of his house visits so that I would be witness to some of the epic verbal battles between him and his friends about the nuisance of the society, the beauty of music and its spiritual undertones, how colors benefit our well-being and how we could use it if we really tried. In fact, Pops strongly believed in free will and choices. He told us that we could do whatever we could imagine with passion and dedication we would fulfill our wildest dreams.

But on these days without him, all I wanted to do was to go outside and catch butterflies with him.

Chapter 8B
The world we live in

"On every surface...you must leave your mark" that was the motto of the land...Tinkkerland to be exact or at least that's what the Mayor keeps harping on.

Made up of multiple cities with different writing, drawing, and marking instruments. What people would call Stationaries Communities. Everything had a specific purpose in this world. But first and foremost we are tools to be of service to the people. They tell us their dreams, and we jot it down whenever they wake up in the morning before it disappears in the routines of their brains. Or we help to sell an idea or product by making visual diagrams. We are there to help solve problems and solidify the process when coming up with the solution, Show me the work.

"Every mark has its purpose and every purpose gets its mark."

We normally come in packs…3, 6, 12, you know multiples…but never just one within the Stationary Community. We live in Gradetler, made up of main pencils of different kinds and functions. They have explained this to us a few times at school, but Pops gave us the real low down.

"Us pencils need to stick together," he would always start,

"…there's all type of stuff out there already dividing us; marking gradients, paint jobs, numbered stamps on our foreheads to identify us to people, mechanicalization (where all the wood is replaced with hard plastic and metal), colored ferrules, different color Caoutchouc or erasers…" - he'd always look at me whenever he'd say that part…

He was preparing me and everyone in the house for what would happen if the other pencils found out about me.

There was a case of this kid who moved into the town Dad and Mom grew up in. There were all kinds of mocking, jeering, thumbtack stuck in their walls with horrible notes, chewed up rubber on the front lawn. And this was from the adults! The kids took their cues from the passive-aggressive teachers, and we all know that kids have no filters especially when they get validations from their peers or the adults. They tortured the little boy for a semester, but no one knew what exactly happened to that kid. His family just up and disappeared, moved away he guessed. Though the parents were normal and somewhat rich, they most definitely could not afford to keep the worse from happening.

As soon as I understood that I was different, I'd hear this story, and this story scared me for years... I was told it in various forms every time I wanted to flex my budding.

Mom especially was overprotective; She and Pops felt I wouldn't quite fit in and would be teased by the other kids. It wasn't like I looked deformed or anything... just incomplete and this made me move a bit slower, my strokes had to be more deliberate. I couldn't just eraser them and start over like everyone else and, naturally I felt left out.

When I was much younger our esteemed Mayor would make us come to the sharpening hut as early as 4 am every time we needed to use it...for our protection he said. Though a limited amount of pencils knew about my condition we still had to be very careful on my excursions.

Mayor Stanford insisted to not cause any dissident between his pencil constituents and have people come into his town looking for a defective pencil. Not on his watch would I be shipped off somewhere in the middle of the night. First, it was eraser hats, but, especially when it gets cold, they would break off easily, 'dry rot' Mom called it. Then there were the plastic capping days.

Yeah, that didn't last long. That might work for those masquerading Mascara pencils, that get to write on people's faces because they were so soft and smudgy. They had to get this transparent cap, so they could tell what color it was from the outside to cover their delicate points.

Day after day, I sat in the basement staring out the small slit window at the other kids leaving their marks on everything they could. I watched Jade, Charc and even Summer leave for school every morning with Mom making a quick back glance now and then…

"Pops, you can make anything right?" - in my best 7 years-old, buttering-up voice. "Why don't you make me a crown that looks like the top of your head? Here I spent all last night drawing the designs for you"

"Oh Scribs…these are…ahh…hard to follow, you really need to slow down…" - he said sheepishly

"…but we can work on it together, it's about time everyone sees how talentedv you can be. Your lines need work, but this is a great idea"

I was like a light-bulb all day working with Pops. Summer even walked by us and Charc came over and wouldn't shut up about how much fun we'll have at school together now, this was going to be so good.

"...and then...you are going to school right?"

Everyone turned and look at Mom...and with a very nervous response she said;

"Fine, I think...hmmm...sure, but you have to check in with me at the library at lunch..."

Chapter 7B
Heart shaped souls

"Strong-willed Dawn, fearless but to a point, nervously precise... She is a striking contradiction... Females aren't supposed to be this domineering..."

These words kept bubbling up in my mind ...that's what pencils said behind my back and the pencils that said that they were just helping would say it to my face...

Followed up with:
"The nerve of some pencils! ... or... "Can you imagine?"

I've battled with this internally and tempered my true self with what people thought I was from I was a kid. Being from a smaller country didn't help matters either. Jumbo pencils in a small case syndrome.

My parents didn't help matters either, they were very protective. They saw my hesitations as fear, not a kid trying to make her mind up and figure out her motivations. No, they thought I was just a delicate flower that they built a 15-acre tinted glass house around.

"Dawn...Dawn! Where did you put my papers?" Slim asked.

"They're in the bottom drawer, underneath the pulp papers," she replied.

That was the last conversation I had with my husband.

As firm and lanky as he was, I wished he'd bend a little... stopped trying to save the world, and saved his world... me and the kids.

I put them first all the time... He didn't need to worry about them, I got that. But why couldn't he show me that he got me...I didn't know where he was.

I knew he was not burning in a wood fire somewhere, nor being chewed up by a rabid dog, yet, I knew he was watching over us somehow, somewhere...but maybe I just...wanted to feel his presence.

Maybe it was that larger than life persona that he gave off...

Everyone loved him....
I loved him from a far before I got to know him...personally.

After that, I just loved him more. I bought shares into his company until I was the vice president.

All the day-to-day running, the contracts, the bribes, the late night negotiations, all the time-consuming stuff fell to me and I understood my role.

I loved it, enjoyed it a bit too much, that's all I wanted to do.

Whoever said love is work knew exactly what they were saying. I loved that my Slim was a dreamer… but in order for him to dream, someone had to keep out the distractions, the noise and all the lights. I was worried that he stayed awake to forget us…his tether to this world, but I knew he was dreaming about us…dreaming for us.

Save this big world for us, but we weren't the only ones living in it, so he had to factor them in too. Now one of them has taken him away from us, away from me.

I wanted him back!

The reason for my purpose…
Since then a new purpose has filled my mind, my work routine has shifted.

Usually, I stretched the work throughout the day. Normally, these kids don't read, underline a word or a sentence. They're too busy tracing their essence on the computer. They were not taking time to learn the full skill it required to build on their lines and shades, putting more and more of themselves on the paper, building up shapes and levels on top of levels, nor stepping back to see an image that could be admired for generations to come.

Even if the people didn't know that it was a family of pencils by the name of Davinci that created those drawings and designs, not the man that owned them.

But we know, we all know…

They are in our history books after all. But these kids can't appreciate that.

There hasn't been a skilled family like that in their lifetime, All they can focus on is the potential of the computer although people were trying to mimic our essence for years and even then, they use us to try and figure that out, stroke after stroke, line after line we create.

Maybe we were just tools to be used after all and since it's getting easier to mimic what comes out of our heart and souls, old tools are all we will be.

"Hey!!, shhhhh…and put that down.
As a matter of fact what are you doing in here, the bell has rung. Get back to class!!"

Chapter 6 B

The secret project...shhh...

Whew.... It's almost time to head home and Mom said I didn't have to wait on her because she had some things to finish up before coming home, but she wouldn't be long and that she better not get there before me or else. As if she had to tell me. I loved having the house to myself even if it was for a little while, no stern screaming, no scoffing and, definitely no Summer yelling. Plus, there's a project I was working on, so I wanted no distractions.

Close your eyes and imagine my house, it looks like the pencil a giant baby would use, with his big grubby hands and fat fingers, a giant baby just learning to write.

Holding it firmly in his fist so he can best control his intentions but still, it comes out as shaky uneven strokes, water marks from the drooling and a crooked bite mark from freshly jotting out teeth. I liked to imagine he was feeling extra confident one day about his writing skills, maybe writing his name or Apple, opting to try instead the big boy three finger way (not the big man two finger way) and wrote what looks more like "h88le",

He'd looked at his best work after multiple tries showed his Pops only to get a pat on the head, you know the one: the uninterested, the stop bothering me one...

"Good boy, now go write Apple..." - his father would say without looking away from his paper.

He shuffled back to the where he was crafting, looked at that paper, cocked his hand all the way to the back of his head and gave that pencil one big fling.... straight out the window. And down and down and down it went, doing an ungracefully somersault destined to find ground to be smashed or stuck.

Luckily for us, it got stuck, in some plush ever-greening lawn grass and in a nice neighborhood. One perfect to raise kids in. Mom and Pops were gliding along one day, found it and now we live in it!

Truth is, Pops designed this house.
He had his heart set on a basement, so he dug deeper in the foundation plot than anyone else and built it himself. But of course, I liked my giant story better.

As quickly as possible, I glided home, down the sidewalk, passing the rubber trimming shop, behind the graphite ice cream store, and I wasn't even tempted once (yay me!), up to our walkway: one, two, three steps...four, five, six...on to the welcome mat...with home scribbled in it! And slammed the door behind me. I tossed my sweaty crown on the kitchen table though Mom would always tell me to be more careful with it, it's not sold in stores after all and I zooped down the stairs down to my secret project.

I got a tan ring around my forehead from wearing that stupid crown all day, I must put it on every time I go outside, even to the put the garbage out.

One day, I was running over to Charc's house to give her back the wood glue, from her last visit. Mom was in one of her "self-sufficient house arrest" moods, and it was early morning so I figured I'd run as fast as I could. In my mind I was like the wind…a hurricane wind, yes a hurricane wind blowing at a comfortable category 5. Yup, I was Scribs the yellow blur.

I wasn't but half way there when I saw a bus filled with preschool stubs heading my way and I thought that's why Yell gets all excited in the mornings…Pops had really picked the perfect spot for the house; it was close to and on route to everything. Mom and Pops weren't the only parent pencils that thought this area was perfect to raise kids in as this was where street a bunch of the preschool pickups was.

No quicker than the thought crossed my mind I felt a draft like a cutting wind on my bare head.

"Oh no, I forgot my crown!" - I whispered, but it seemed I screamed it because immediately all eyes were looking this way.

I hid in the bushes that separated the two houses. The dirt wasn't too tasty and it didn't help that it was wet either.

It must have been 20mins before I was missed at home although I think it was more about the crown resting on the countertop next to the drawer Mom kept everything in. I was rescued by Miss Bubble Belly, who was quite quiet, I didn't even feel her get down beside me, putting the crown on my head

"Forgot something Scribsy?" She asked.

"You know you have to be more careful; Mom's on the paranoid path and I'm not that fond of living in a hole...again" (grin) I guess she can be nice on a rare occasion.

Back to my secret project.

So I pulled out the canvas from below the stacks of paper Pop had stored for use when he takes work home. The whiteness pushing from the darkness of the basement almost blinded me with all its brilliance...Oh the possibilities!

I lay it out on the ground and just dug in...I instinctively went to the left edge of the paper, I'm not sure why I always started there but I always did, felt very comfortable, like it's a life rule or something, then I swayed to the right. Then I glided up, down, left right, 90 degree, 45...circles, squares. Long, medium, short strokes, rocked and tilted back and forth, leaned forward and back, mark after mark, stroke after stroke matched each of the four sides. A kaleidoscope of shapes began to form, thickness and thinness of lines separated each other as if they were choosing sides in a family feud. My trance continued until very little white space remained. By the time I stopped, I faintly heard mom calling from upstairs…

"Scribs honey…. Scribsy…."

Oh no, what time is it? I didn't hear any of the usual commotions of Mom and Summer getting home. Time must have jetted by. I thought what if she saw this, she'd become even more protective. I didn't want to be more of a weirdo. I just started to get a friend, not a family sanctioned friend, one who chose me. I was thinking I could share my secret with because it was eating me up inside having this gift and not being able to show anyone. And now Mom would certainly lock me away, I know she loves me…but sometimes it's too much. I had to think fast, and then it happened…

I started to spin…around and around, forming a spiral on the ground and I felt the spiral syncing with my thoughts, and with each turn everything came into place…dash, space, dash, space, dash, space, dash….

I was invisible??

"Scribs?"

"Scribbles?"

"Scribbles St. Mark Pastelle?"

"I could have sworn I heard him down here a while ago, I told him to head straight home after school, I tell you that boy is becoming his father…"

"Whew, that was close."

Wait, what just happened, what did I just do?

I figured out that sometimes I'll be there writing, and these patterns begin to form, …but I never thought it could go this far…never dreamed it. And why hasn't this ever happened before?

"I…I…I…'m just as confused as anyone"

Before I got into real trouble, I had to figure out a way to let Mom know I'm here and I've been here…

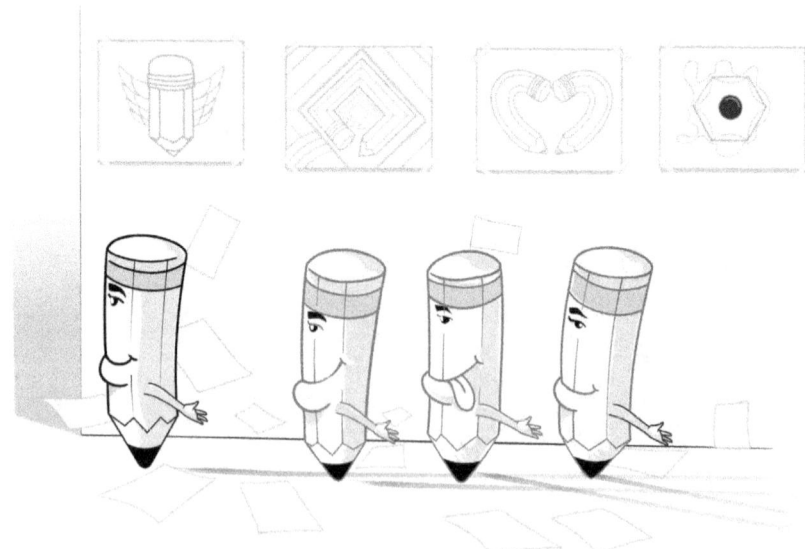

Chapter 5B
Jaded...I hope your mother doesn't find out.

"Where…where…sniff…where have you been? I was worried sick, I felt like I had swallowed lead, although we were never made of lead and this isn't ancient Rome, and I'm not even sure what a stylus is…but I was sickened to my hollowed out core. It felt as if my life force was being evaporated with worry."

I heard Mom shouting through the sobs. She always rambled and spewed elaborate trivia when she was upset. But she got quiet when she was really, really upset.

I ran up the stairs, making my myself dizzy in the process, going round and round those stairs made me feel like a corkscrew being yanked out of a wine bottle and all that air left my body as if it was a bit of wine would spilling out Mom and Pop drank when they were relaxing at home after work. As I ascended the last step into the bright lights of the kitchen, I saw a plate of food was on the counter covered with a mesh bonnet, the darkness of the graphite beamed thru but it was cold as steel. Yell's high chair was empty, the kitchen was spotless and sterile, quiet and eerie like a hospital room at 3 am right before a bus load of accident victims began to pile in and all hell breaks loose.

I realized after Mom said, "…worry" she didn't say anything else, and I saw that she was turning orange and that tint was getting darker heading to red, much like one of those color changing hot wheels toy cars. She was resting on the stool directly in front of the counter and her point was digging into the floor, the scuff marks were now designs etched into the tiles. She was furious!

Jade was standing across from her, with the same look on her face, but the less intense, not often expressed, "teenagey" version. No this wasn't built up anger, but a defiant and "stand-my-ground"-ey anger.

It was after 10 p.m.…How did I know that? Because Mom said it when the back door first opened letting in a gleam of light that quietly rushed into the kitchen making itself at home with all the boastfulness of a Jamaican after the Olympics, and hid just as fast when the door was closed. Mom flicked on the light to show her pale wet cheeks getting back its color as her anger built.

"So you're not going to explain yourself, young lady?"

"I….I…I got nothing…I could tell you the truth, that it was my fault and all, but what's the point, you're still gonna get mad and put on your warden uniform and lock us in this hole you call a house for as long as it takes for the food to run out or for the cabin fever to set in?" Jade mumbled.

"Oh well. Since you know that, why did you come back to the hell hole then? Why'd you come back to this prison, where you get three square meals a day, fresh clothes, a comfy bed and, an education? Maybe I should lock you in the basement and only feed you once a day? How about that for a prison?"

"I feel like I can't talk to you anymore, this is why Pops left...you..."

Smack!

She stumbled back and took a while to catch her balance. Jade's jaw got bigger than usual...and it was now as red as Mom's anger was. She began to form something with her lips...but it just couldn't come out. I wanted to go and hug her around her waist, so she could rub her eraser in my back as she did. Yet, I couldn't help to think...well, that was unexpected...she said nothing after that.

Was this part of growing up and getting older, as your wood gets tight around your ferrule, you feel defiant and you want to stretch out and exercise your growing strength? Mom's reaction was expected. I'm surprised she took so long actually. But as much as my sister bugged me, her talking to Mom like that was not in the cards.

I snuck off to my room as soon as I caught my composure.

I had recently talked my way out of my little "disappearing act" down in the basement earlier. It was a good thing Charc was home and not off at some journalistic note taking class. I had snuck out and ran over there now freshly crowned (I wasn't going to let that happen again), I didn't let her get a word in edge wise asking her to cover for me by saying that I was there all this time. I convinced Charc to say that she called me as soon as I got into the house.

It was a good thing Mom didn't see the crown that had fallen on the floor when I tossed it across the kitchen counter. I would have been in very serious trouble.
But now, all that had shifted, an invisible sand line had been crossed between Jade and Mom. It looked more like a tripwire because Mom just exploded.

They had a very long discussion that night, which really meant that Mom spoke and answered sometimes, while Jade was silent for the rest of the time. As I got ready for school the next morning, I passed her bedroom door, Jade was still whimpering. The house was quiet for the next couple of days, even my favorite loud-mouth sister Summer picked up on something. It was like bubble wrap and eggshells all over the house.
But funnily, it wasn't "lock down" central.

Other than this obvious tension, things ran as smoothly as it could. Well, the daily routine stayed on track: home, school, work, kindergarten, basement, and the occasional yelling for food.

But then other activities were added: the almost inaudible sobbing behind a locked teen rap group poster plastered door and a quiet dinner table.

Jade wasn't officially grounded; it was more implied and expected. She came home right after school and just locked herself in her room and cried. I wasn't sure what exactly she was crying for. Was it the disrespect she showed mother? Or was it that she felt she had to speak her mind? Either way, it put a damper on the house for a while, and I didn't like it.

A couple of days later, we found out the truth... well, I would. I knew I couldn't get into Jade's room whenever she got home, but this strange behavior had been gnawing at my flats and edges, with all that crying, timidity and most of all not eating. I knew something was up. You thought I'd be happier about this, but it felt too weird to revel in the peace and quiet. I mean I got plenty of time alone down in the basement, but all I did was think about what had happened. A proper line was not formed just swirls in pretty much the same place.

So the next day, I convinced Mom I wasn't feeling well. Because of our patterns in the mornings, I knew exactly when she'd realize that I wasn't where I was supposed to be, and that she'd come to check on me. I placed a flashlight right up to my forehead until I was sweating a bit, then put on my best sickly look and voice.

"Scribs! Why are you not eating your breakfast? You know we'll be 4 minutes and 35 seconds late if you don't hurry up."

I heard her annoyance getting louder as she got to the door.

"Mommyyyy, I don't feel too good... I think I have a fever."

"Yes, you do feel hot, but that could be that you've been laying in the hot room all morning" - she snapped back quickly.

"Since I woke up, I felt as if I wanted to throw up a couple of times." - I whimpered.

"Ok, I don't have much time to go through all of this with you, I'll be back to check on you at lunch time, you know the rules, don't go outside, stay away from the windows unless your crown is on and don't stay in that musty basement all day," - she stated while walking out of the room.

It took 10 minutes of shuffling and banging around before all was quiet…Everyone had left.

I waited 10mins for everything to be completely quiet, and double-checked to see that no one was running back because they forgot something.

Then I ran down to the kitchen, grabbed a smothered graphite slice and headed back up to Jade's room.

I pushed the shut door. Jade must have suspected something, or she was hiding something, because I had to really lean in to open that door, and it opened just wide enough to be ajar.

I slipped in to find that behind the door a waist-high pile of clothes was blocking it. But it didn't look like anything else was out of place the room was quite clean and neat. Piles of girly magazines, conditioner, and softener caps so that her eraser didn't get dry and crack up on the dresser, inspirational posters of rap, reggae and pop songwriting pencils in various stages of hung on the walls, though I didn't think the latter did much writing, they just repeat words like ohhh, ahhh and whoa.

I have been in here a couple of times to pick up or drop off stuff Mom asked me to, but I never quite took stock of what was actually in here. All I saw was pink so I would drop off what I needed to and left.

Now, I spun around a couple of times...slowly of course, thinking:

"What's really going on with Bubble Belly?"

And as I was about to leave defeated, thinking how I was missing today's technical drawing class, I saw a bowl of soft served graphite cream, and underneath it was a notebook with a couple of pages torn out and some jottings on the front.

"A clue, yes this is getting good" I bellowed so loudly I startled myself a bit.

"Hehehe…I knew she was hiding something. But what was it?"

The impressions on the page were faint and, about 4 pages were missing. But I could make out a bunch of random numbers. I sat there for a bit and then an idea hit me.

I ran downstairs and back up as fast as I could with a bit of paper in hand, the see-through kind that would make what you were looking at was much brighter provided that you stared long enough.

I placed this paper on both sides of the notebook page to cover my tracks, tilted away to the side and just rubbed my point back and forth until it covered the whole page, then I took the notebook and returned it to where I found it, very carefully. I piled back up the clothes as much as possible, pulled back this "teenagey door", swore to myself that I'd never been like this and glided back to the basement to try and figure out what were the bunch of numbers I was looking at.

"679. 887: 709. 227, 569N. 485SE: 237. 094…. I really hope your mother doesn't find out"

"…I hope your mother doesn't find out?"

Chapter 4B
A hot point...

Mom came home and found me lying in bed with the covers up over my head.

"Oh, I didn't expect that now you're soaked with sweat."

I was so tired, and I was getting sick now.

I spent the last couple hours before lunch racking my brain trying to figure out what this note meant and what

Jade knew.

And now I was sick with questions.

Was she out searching for Pops the other night?

Did she already have this note before he left?

Is this why he left?

Where are you Pops?

What's going really on?

Why am I so nosey?

Chapter 3B
Buried treasure?

I slept most of the day but not well, there were too many questions in my mind, and after the long nap, I knew I wouldn't get rid of them.

The next day, the whole morning routine was a quiet blur. If things happened I didn't notice. I was too much in my head. It was the same at school too. Whether we were going to be these things or not it was required...another hard-line was drawn by the mayor.

Letter writing class...for those to be placed in office careers, Numbers writing class...for the potential mathematicians, Cursive writing...for the budding romantic poets, Images...doodling, artist and artisans

Break!

Finally, as much as my mind floated all over the place I didn't forget to eat. Mom packed a hearty lunch of graphite soup with clay balls and Caoutchouc bread for dipping, mom keeps saying I should eat it all up, every last bit, because it will make my point grow big, strong and hard. The more clay in your diet, the harder your point gets and the fainter your impression on this whole white world of the technical industry.

I was not sure why she made me bring lunch and meet with her at break time, I had stopped eating with her a year ago.

Mom wanted me to end up as a draft pencil that focused on technical line drawings. They're more rigid, calculated and made fewer mistakes. And they always had a dedicated jumbo eraser partner assigned to them., so my lack of an eraser wouldn't be a problem then.

We didn't see much of the "Rubbers"; they're from the next town over, and we only met up during office hours in the big city offices or the occasional founders' picnic here in town, which Pops used to organize with the help of the whole family. Even Yell didn't mind sharing the attention of Pop's friends and co-workers.

"Are you going to have that, mate?" the voice came from right over my head.

"Nope, you know I have no use for them, they're mostly for show and Mom's defiant optimism" I retorted. "Plus you always steal them anyway, I just pretend not to see when you do it…Berol!"

"Yeah, yeah…mumble mumble…what's with those numbers you wrote in class by the way?" he snapped back.

"What numbers?" – I asked with wide eyes while sheepishly looking at my betraying point.

"You didn't even notice what you were writing in Letter Writing class, did you?"

Actually, I didn't really remember anything, but the numbers from yesterday so when Berol called it out I figured that's what he was talking about.

"Don't worry though, I rubbed them out for you when no-one was looking" - he said before stuffing rubber bread in his mouth hole. "So is that our new code? 'Cause I didn't get any of what you were trying to tell me." - he continued to mumble.

I had to think quickly. Did I want to add anyone else to this mystery? How would I pull it off? How was I going to solve this myself? But then I'd have to give him the whole story, how would I even explain it?

"Well yeah, …it's…a…new…."

"Scribs, you took too long to answer, I could see the wheels in your head turning…I'll leave it for now, but are you going to finish that?"

That's my best friend, well I would say he's becoming one of my best friends, but I didn't have many friends… Missing preschool did that.
He's the only one at school that knew about my eraser problem. Well, lack thereof.

I came to school one day and there he was this kid taking over my "newbie" spot for two months of kids picking on me, and the proof was all my smudges from being bumped into all the time. Mostly, kids would bump into me. But other times, I would bump into them as I never looked where I was going because I was staring down at the floor trying to avoid all the attention.

I couldn't tell if the looks it were "the regular"; "Why'd he start so late in the school year?", "Who's this kid getting special treatment because his Mom works here now?" or the "What is that on your head?"

The looks went on for a couple of weeks before it felt as if it was only the: "What's that on his head?" looks. Well I was self-conscious, looking for outside validation, even though I did trick Charc the first time that Pops made it.

I went over her house pretending to be lost, but she figured it out a little bit after I started talking. I could see the puzzled look on her uncertain skinny face. She did say she couldn't tell even up close. I still would wonder if everyone could tell, I mean being at school every day was the ultimate test.
2 months 2 days later...

"Hi, my name is Berol Aquamarine the third, I just moved here from the motherland England, you look like a mate that sat in the back of my 1st-grade class back in primary, bruv."

"Yeah hey Berol, you said your name and where you were from this morning in class remember and I don't like playing the "you look like someone other than my family" game"

"Well the name is Scribbles, right? I was trying to make small talk but...what are you really hiding under that crown on your head, bruv?"

"What are you going on about n..ow?" - I shot back.

"Yeah, I noticed your lines are not quite perpendicular a bit around here..." he illustrated on his head, "and I figured I'd come and ask you to be certain."

"Where'd you see that? Not all of us can be perfect like you, you know? Everyone has a crown by the way..." I said turning to walk away.

"Yes, but yours starts an inch below the first ring. I wasn't too sure what it was, but I knew something was off and it would drive me crazy for the rest of my time here; however long before Father move us again," - he paused.

"...My mother said I should be completely honest when I'm trying to make friends if it's meant to be, then they won't see my words as too harsh, and if they do they'll respect me for at least truly being myself." - he dryly continued.

That day I found out how meticulous Berol could be, all the time we were talking…he was there checking out my lines, the measurement of my ferrule ratio, the grips that kept an eraser intact, how seamless everything straightens up or not. I went on trying to convince him differently for all of 10mins before I gave up and told him to meet me right after school, when everyone was rushing out the door when we'd have 5mins of privacy. He didn't seem that anxious or excited that he was about to get his nagging question answered or the revelation that he had caught me in a lie.

"So, what is it?" – he asked as he walked into the bathroom.

"I have to show you, but it has to be quick, lock the door I don't want anyone else knowing."

"You were right I am wearing a crown…"

"I know that…well, whatever you call it…my question is why?"

"I'm about to show you…will you shut up!" - as I pulled the crown off. I continued, "I have no eraser, I don't even have a ring to hold it in even if I did grow one 2 years from now"

I saw his eyes widen, iris contracting back into his skull like reversing into a dark tunnel.

"Oh…I thought it was something silly like a different color or half being trimmed off by some overzealous barber… But that's cool."

"That's cool?"

Yeah one less thing to do, now all you have to do is sharpen your point and you're good."

"Well…yeah…good point…never really thought of that."

From that day he's always been the one that brought me back into perspective. It's not like we hung out everyday…because of you Mom having one of her episodes, but when we did I always seemed to go back on the right track and he'd always seem to know when I'm veering off. We became more alike the more we hung out or maybe he was trying to be more "American".

"So Scribs, what were those numbers, some girl's phone number, a password you set up last night or coordinates?"

"Coordinates, Berol you're a genius!"

Why didn't I think of that before! Yes! That made perfect sense. Pops wouldn't be cheating on Moms and be writing numbers in a home note pad, knowing how 'nuff' (curious) Jade and Summer were I figured that's what Jade was doing why she came home so late the other night. She probably looked up the number in the phone directory, found the address then went to check out what happened or at least she tried to see our Daddy again. It might have taken her a while to get there and back or just overwhelmed her so that she couldn't face home... especially Mom.

"Are we going hunting for buried treasure or something? - Berol asked.

"We sure are...tomorrow night!"

Chapter 2B

What we do in the dark...

Why?

Why?

Why?

Why?

Why did I tell Berol we were going out tomorrow night? The furthest I'd snuck out to was next door, which mostly didn't end well for me, so how the heck was I going to get to the other side of town to Pensvilletown?

Right after we had that revelation, we went up to the Principal's office on to "the Google", as some old pointers call it at times, and put the numbers in the map app and it zoomed in to an area outside of Pensvilletown. This place as far as we knew was empty like a blank sheet of paper made out of recycled banana leaves, off colored and slightly bumpy, you know that type of paper people used to print "news" on? We used it when we're just get our writing bearings on the grips of a crafted finish. No one really knew what's out there. Then it clicked! Pops would bring back some expensive paper from Pensvilletown.

"I wonder if that's where they had your Pops working on a top-secret mission, that he couldn't tell anyone about not even mom, and they locked him in this huge top secret underground bunker, while they built this huge rocket shaped ship thingy that could catch and hold all types of aliens, crayons and markers from other boxes, and they took things and placed them in the Everything Store Zoo for everyone to be in awe of, gawk at and poke with their grubby fingers. You know how warped and bent out of shape humans can get?" - Berol reeled off like a politician trying to win new votes.

"B, I know you're not that fond of people, but not all of them are the same, pops worked side by side with one, he's been cool. They're "Per-cils" for point's sake." - I mumbled."

"Per-cil? That's dumb…isn't that singular, and there's not even a pronoun anywhere near that silly attempt to be inclusive." - Berol blurted out.
He was about to launch into one of his famous tangents but I cut him off with…

"You can be such a pencil case at times…"

Now how am I going to get out?

Mom tended to go to bed earlier of late, because Jade is home and Summer usual tires herself out whining about food or crying herself to sleep. Pops normally stayed up and played with her till she fell asleep, then he'd go down to do some work or just go to bed with Mom. But I guess everyone was feeling the void. Now Jade was the one I had to worry about…all of those times I've snuck out she always knew or was right there when I got back as if she placed a tracker on me or something. So I'd to be careful and map this out properly. I'd already included B, so I couldn't get anyone else involved. Especially not "Ms Loudmouth McGee" next door although it would be nice to have back up. But I didn't want the world to know. I'm pretty sure she was the leak who told Jade, maybe not intentionally, but she just can't keep her trap shut.

I wrote out my plan, labelling it: "The After 8pm Dash" It laid out what I needed, routes I could take, how long it would take, etc…

I placed it in an old storybook I read when I was younger, and I left it on the table as I made a quick dash to the basement. In the basement I paced back and forth, talked to myself while I thought about this plan. I was sure to lock the door this time, because I didn't want any more surprises when I got stressed and lost in thought.

"…Leave right after dinner, leave one of my crowns out so they'll think I'm still here…meet up with B at the end of town…But how are we going to get there? What route should I take there? One that has the least amount of light possible which passes the sharpening station…they may or usually shut it down at 8…right? –

Yup, he would normally be there later at the request of moms, so I could be sharpened after I overzealously rub down my point…"

"Yeah, so he shouldn't be a problem, after all I'm as fast as lightning when I want to be…"

"You sure are." –

"Damn right…high five" –

Slap!

"Hold on, did I just high five myself?"

"You sure did, but next time take it easy or do a mental one!"

"What???"

I startled myself… "Where the heck did you come from?"

"I've been walking behind for the last five minutes…well pacing."

"Yeah, but where did you come from?"

"Isn't it obvious…You drew me. While you were pacing and thinking you didn't notice you drew the answer to your questions. Well one huge question… How are you going to get out of this? Now here I am…I can't tell you exactly how it works, quantum physics and some other mumbo jumbo."

"But…but..but….", I mumbled as I stared at this thing that looked like me, that's saying I drew it.

"Now are you ready to do this?"

So, I snuck out through the back door with a backpack filled with snacks, a map, and scraps of paper, that I folded up neatly at the bottom of the bag...you know, just in case.

I looked left, right and right again. Charc's house was dark except for her mom's room light. She was at a desk with her head titled down, her glasses gleamed with hard reflections from those plastic rims, almost like sharp darts shooting outside the window. It reminded me to check Jade's window as well...I didn't believe she'd be in there laying in the dark, wrestling with her thoughts.

She's not that type. I figured she's binding her time until her curiosity got the best of her and she attacked it, like a freshly cut cake, with a slice of it was already missing, why not devour the rest of it? I had to beat her to it if I wanted to get any of it.

It was ghostly on these narrow streets after 9 pm the trails of the day melded and smudged together, so you couldn't tell where one line started and another began. There were fat lines, skinny lines, soft lines, hard lines, swirly and broken lines, the broken lines were from uncertain kids, not sure of the type of markings they left out there in the world. The swirly ones tended to come from the carefree artistic types, soft-tipped, but confident to try other ways.

As I followed the lines and my map, I came across Berol on a bench sitting under a street pole half in the light. He didn't see me coming, or at least that's what I thought, for he looked so comfortable being in the open air at night.

"Took you long enough, bruv"

"Well it's my first time, I'm using a map!"

"And why do you look like you've been here a lot, does your Dad know where you are?"

"No, he most definitely doesn't, now let's go find yours…"

Chapter 13
The musings of a powerful point

I had often found myself being pulled in different directions. It seemed I had to be in four places at once. Respect and power are one thing, but entitlement and expectations are another. It dragged me back to my childhood mindscape, growing without much understanding and point hold, fueled with the embarrassment of being different, odd, strange, weird. And those were a few of the things I heard people refer to me as, whether to my face or my back. I didn't have to pivot too far before someone launched into their child abomination rant, or it was passed out in pamphlets on the streets in town.

How to Shame and Humiliate Kids - the Family Edition. A great read for the entire family, and it even came with a practice words template. I must have heard them a thousand times before I learned to stop listening. Even though that decision came with its life lessons. It helped me to cope, develop, plot, build…confidence, a little…. Or was it for some nice cold oats porridge-revenge?

My son doesn't know my true nature, how could he? He's at two forearms length and a bit out of reach.

He's a Mama's boy. Always wrapped up in hugs, trying to get away from my personality, but occasionally I have reached in to test the waters…see how he's developing before I grab him away and give him the other side of life that his mom has been shielding him from.

"He's just a child, let him be my baby for a while longer." she always says.

To which I responded - "Well, I'll give you five more minutes, and remember my watch is fast!"

Technically, we're still in that 5mins, but when it ends, he's mine to teach and bring up in the ways of a Stanford Pencil. I will teach him that we Stanfords make bold marks wherever we go no matter the circumstance, no matter the surface and no matter the page.

He's lucky to have me as a father, a strong hard edge who is proud of his heritage all the way back the motherland, England.

I've studied our lineage and saw how powerful, pure and true our family name was and still is. We were the first set of pencils made from the discovery of that graphite rock mine and we've been maintaining traditions of purpose, power, and traditions ever since.

And I need him to understand that...This is the place he needs to strive for and, the longer his Mom keeps him from it the bigger the feat will be when he assumes his role in our family's history. Until that time comes, I still have work to do.

My strong standing has been somewhat threatened by an upstart, spouting his modern ideas of equality and freedom to create one's destiny. Blah blah blah...Black sheet!

But he just upped and disappeared one day... Where? That's not important right now, what's important is that I'm here at the top, trying to run a small pencil town out in suburbia that's beneath me. But I have a bigger sheet of paper to rip.

We will return to England one day, as conquerors!

Normally Mayors would have their office in the middle of town, where everyone can have access to their every need, query and compliant. But I moved out here at the edge of town. I rather like my space and it gives my subjects...I mean residents, literal space to think about things before they run it down to my office. I mean, how long does it take to realize a separate sidewalk for rubber pets makes no sense and is a waste of money?

But they believe that I am the first line of defense to shield the citizens from the potential bad that comes into our town from time to time.

What is he doing here so late at night, and with a backpack at that? Where is he going? Is he running away?

"Hey, Kid...stop, you shouldn't be out here this late!" – I shouted

As soon as he came across my window, he vanished, and then another...deep in the darkness of the night. I couldn't quite make out the other kid, but I knew it was two of them. Then I thought, that first kid's mother wouldn't even let him go to school without her, and I suggested especially since the recent disappearances that they all move to another town and start over. So how would he be this far out at night, with some other kid, I'm sure he does have any friends.

He must be in trouble, I must call his house and check. I wouldn't think everything could go downhill this fast, from one person's absence.

Ring…

Ring…

Ring….

Ring…….

"H…He…Hello, How may I help you at this time of night?"

"Good Night, sorry to be calling this late..but…"

"No you're not…just spit it out, sir…Mayor"

"Well Mrs. Pastelle, ever since your husband left, is it that everyone over there would start wandering the streets late at night? Why don't you keep a tighter leash on your son?"

"What are you talking about now? No, he's in his room…you are most definitely mistaken…"

"But have you checked to see if he's actually in there? I did wake you…so you're answering off faith, something amiss is going on other there"

"Excuse you?- You don't think I know where my kids are at night, what type of mother do you think I am?" - Mrs. Dawn Pastelle shot back.

"Listen Dawny...eh...I mean Mrs. Pastelle, I'm not questioning your abilities as a mother, it's obvious to me that you need help, I just saw something so I'm checking it out..."

"You know what, I'm finished having this conversation." – she said cutting him off.

"Wow...well that went....eh...weller than usual."

Chapter HB
Where the all points meet

"Where the hell are we?"

"Who's bright idea was it to search for coordinates at night?"

There was nothing but pitch-black things out here-pitch-black walls, pitch-black trees, pitch-black halls, then pitch-black grass...And then as I turned around slowly to an even more pitch blacker night air. I know you can't see air, but you couldn't see anything else. It was just black. I could take my crown off and shine a light off my shiny dome head but it wouldn't matter. This darkness eats light. Every time I turn on the flashlight I would hear, Gulp! We'd only seen small pockets of lights ever since we ducked and passed the Mayor's office. I didn't even know why he's this far out here. I didn't even notice when Berol took off. That boy moved faster than a hard pencil point on plastic-coated paper. At times I wondered if he just teleported. No wonder his points stayed so sharp.

Either way, I think we are in the right spot. Or we are completely lost.

Where were we?

What's my doppelgänger doing? ....I...I can't allow my mind to wander too much...I'm still not sure how all this works...but I was not ready to be on "Rubber-less Pencil Cases Got Talent" if these things started popping out every time my mind started to drift.

"Scribs, what are you doing?"

"Are you sure this is the spot, why are you gliding back and forth talking to yourself?

"No I'm not, but what spot? Do you...Can you see anything around here?"

"No, but I can hear something mechanical comin..."

As soon as the air ate the last g that came out of his mouth, a blinding beam of light shot up in the air, and we both started to glow. Then all the insects started to dance around like drunken and confused dust particles. The low rubble got louder and louder. A light got brighter and hotter. Smoke dispersed all over the place. I couldn't see with all the light, smoke and noise. My brain told me to get out of there and stay where I was at the same time, I was frozen.

I felt my point had made up its mind up and started moving to the furthest bush cover it could get to... pushing into Berol and carried him in my path to safety.

Then something shot out into the hazy star speckled darkness. Up! Up! And formed a ninja star that faded away. Was this my first rocket ship? We don't have any space exploration in these parts...but I knew that mark...I'd seen it somewhere before. The bright burning light scared away all the pitch blackness to reveal the full shape of this observatory, the gleaming relative glass, dome shape, counted bricks, a perfect place to look up and watch the lightshow of the stars.

"Wow, did you see that Scribs, did you? I was right...I was right!"

"Shhhh...quiet down, I'm right beside you Berol, I was the one that stopped you from being burnt to charcoal...I didn't stop to look at the large vessel that shot out of the ground."

"Yeah, yeah, whatever, Why didn't you tell me your Dad was into this cool stuff too? I'm so glad we came to look for...wait..."

It hit us and we rushed to where the light shot out from and there it was nothing again...just pitch blackness and heat. We spun around, paced back and forth, left and right until the floor was cold to the touch, but we couldn't find an entrance, an opening...nothing!

One thing was for sure this place was as well-hidden as a Christmas present you bought about 2 months earlier, where you hid it so well you hid it from yourself. We wandered around for at least 15mins. Then we decided the discovery of a space exploration portal was enough, and started to head home. It was way past our bedtime, and the longer we stayed out would be very close to our "death" time.

The glide back was much shorter, the Mayor office light was off, so he must have gone home. Since it was a weekday everyone else had done so also. I'd spent a couple of nights visiting the sharpening station to know how these streets can be, so getting home was a breeze. Berol and I chatted the whole way about the ship and what that could mean for our little town, how likely it was that aliens existed. What they'd look like. How they would be treated, and if we'd get to meet them.

"Maybe just maybe, I could go visiting a new earth for a summer break or two, I'd save up all my lunch money and all the money from Grandma Xmas cards and eat space graphite ice cream" - Berol spewed out.

"That would be great…" - I would chime in from time to time, trying not to reveal my real thoughts…

How was dad mixed up in all of this? How was I going to get in the house? And how was I going to get rid of this clone?

When I got home it was pitch black. Less pitch black than the launch site, but darker than I remembered or expected. There was no stirring, no lights under the back-kitchen door, no gleam in the basement glass, no dull aching light of someone fighting to maintain a level of anger, patience, and sleep.

I gently ran my tip slowly to the door, placing my ear to it as to ear what... I'm not sure. As I was backing away I thought I heard a click and a tight squeeze slowly turning the doorknob as if not to disturb the quietness of the tired, sleepy neighborhood.

I was a bit startled but not too much, I was expecting it, I was caught....

What story could I tell?

Whatever it was, I wasn't going to tell the truth.
It was one of those "too hard to believe - don't want to incriminate others - long stories" that I wasn't finished with, so I couldn't even explain with any confidence to prove I wasn't lying.

"Oi, you coming in or not"- the voice quickly startled me out of thought.

"I might just be the one that gets into trouble, but I've grown a bit fond of you so get in here before you end up with your point broken and you be labeled a "pencil-case.""

"Whew, I thought you were Jade and I was just thinking that pencil case bit..." - I mumbled out

"Yeah, yeah…we are kinda connected and I'll be gone by morning or as soon as you learn to focus your skill, I've served my purpose. That's how this works…" - he said as we went our separate ways, I went to my room and he went to the basement.

I was kind of tired after I got in last night, but still on edge thinking there's no way no one noticed I was missing last night. I went all the way to the edge of another town, had a rocket ship shot at my head, saved my best friend from being a crispy point *(I guess I'll have to elevate him now)*, roamed in the street late at night trying not to be noticed, and got back into a fortress of a house that I have no keys for, then tried to go to sleep with a mental realization of myself wandering in the basement leaving scuff marks everywhere and touching all my stuff. Then I got up before everyone woke up and made sure he was right that he had truly disappeared in the morning *(as soon as I figure how all this works I'll explain it)*

"Hi Jade, how's my favorite sister, would you like some of my breakfast?"

"What do you want Squirt?" - she blurted out unlike someone that hadn't spoken in months.

"Nothing, just checking in on my sweet older sibling figure" - with the most buttery voice I could muster.

(Rolling her eyes) "I'm fine, Scribs now stop talking and hand over the food."

"How was your night, what did you get up to my sister?" - with my eyes fluttering like an awning in the evening breeze.

"Ah...I came home....(nom nom)...ate dinner... (nom nom) then went to bed...weren't you right here... (nom nom)..." – she said in between bites

"Cool, cool..."

As my voice trailed off, I was thinking I had gotten my answer. It didn't feel like she knew anything; then she blurted out:

"Why'd you ask me that though..." - spitting out some food

"Nothing, just making conversation."

"Oh...ok, annoying much?"

And she said nothing else, not another peep, which was odd for Jade.

Maybe I was just missing her torturing bigger sistering ways, it was a week now. I expected things to go back to the way it was by now. I wondered if anything would ever be the same again. Pops was missing for whatever reason, Mom was overprotective and prone to fly off the handle at any time, Jade was docile - I could say pretty much anything to her and she shrugged it off and even Summer seemed to be less "bawly"- not quiet- but less wailing. Had my family dynamic changed for the better? Could I expect it to change again soon? Was I growing up? What were we now?

Not to mention these skills…what was that, was it all a dream?

"Where were you last night, Scribsy?" - Mom said as she appeared into the kitchen with Summer in tow.

"I…I ….I was in bed! ….What? I was in bed…yes in bed Ma!!"

"As I figured. I got a strange call last night that you were out in the street, I even went to check on you last night, in my….(yawn)…sleepy state."

"I must have a goofy twin you guys didn't tell me about, Ma." - with a nervous chuckle.

"Maybe…, You kids go on without me, I'll see you later at school. I haven't woken up properly and I have to have a talk with that obnoxious Mayor of ours…this is getting out of hand now."

I caught Jade's eyes locked on me, puzzled and concerned. I could hear her saying "Goofy twin? … What's going on?"

Chapter F
Pencil shavings....?

What's going on indeed?

If you thought my morning started oddly, it didn't get any better, Berol didn't show up for school. I got a visit from the Mayor asking when was the last time I saw his son, Berol?

"Why do you look so surprised, he didn't tell you who his father was?"

"No....no sir..."

"Well that's strange..."

"Did something bad happen to Berol, Sir?... Sir?

"Oh no...no my dear boy, we're trying to work out some logistics that's all, I'm concerned about his behavior and his influences of late, and I received some reports, which might be unrelated, of some kids vandalizing some private property right on the cusp of the next town. They found a pin his Grandmark gave him at the site, and a book with some funny looking drawings. I know he doesn't draw, I won't allow it... So I'm trying to match the symbols with the personality I guess..." - he paused

"You know anyone like that?" - he asked as if he already knew the answer.

"No…not really, Sir. There's a bunch of kids that could fit that role in our art class. I'll look out for them sir. I'm late for class, so I have to run" - I said as I glided off, not waiting for a response.

I had to get out of there, my face was giving away more than I wanted it to. I was in full brain-lost-think mode. No wonder he was acting funny when we saw the light was off in the Mayor's office on the way back, but I didn't have a clue it was his father. He never brought it up and I didn't care to ask who his father was really. I had my own father issues.

But most importantly, I had to rush back to class to check my backpack. And sure enough, my doodle pad wasn't there. I had taken it out to check if we were in the right coordinated spot, but I'm sure I hadn't put it back, it must have fallen out when we were trying not to get burnt to a crispy mark…With all my worrying about the clone and rushing to get home, I didn't even miss it. I'm not dumb enough to put my thoughts down on paper I track around with me all the time. Do you know who my sisters are? But I did have the coordinates in there, and the Mayor can trace the personality of a pencil by how they make their strokes and lines. Luckily, I had mostly mimicked Pops fluid expressions…but…

"Oh Pencil shavings!!"…I gulped

Chapter 2H
Can pencils be zombies..?

"Oh, there's Jade now…"

Something weird was going on in the house… Well weirder than usual, since Pops disappeared. I found myself wondering around school with things on my mind. More than how my emerald skin looks with this scarf, or how puffy my pink hair looks, or how rosy my cheeks look…the mark of a girl with a healthy eating habit.

"Hey, Jade I haven't seen you after school much. We miss you…there are a lot more donuts left at the store though…hehehe"

"Jade, where have you been? Is the food circus in town? The "All-we-can-try-&-feed-you-buffet?"
"When are you rejoining the team, you don't know what's at steak?"

"Having 4 slices of pizza in your pockets for a mid morning, noon, afternoon & before dinner snack doesn't qualify you for the student council strategic planning team…"

I get it, I'm fat!

Fatter than most, I eat my fair share and a bit more. I'm a chubby pencil, perfect for first graders to grip their small hands around. I'm not very active, and I don't hide it. I'm also proud and will not shy away from my vices, but why are these fat jokes and puns hurting more and more?

They used to just roll off my back...my greasy back but now...Now I'm doing them too?
Either way, I'm more irritable and not as hungry; my mind is full of other thoughts and Mom all alone. She's putting on a straighter braver face, but I can see her shade has faded a bit.

A couple of months ago, she was beaming.
So much that I thought we were getting another brother. It's how her soul would light up when we hung out, when she kissed Scribs in the mornings, when she would rock Summer to sleep at nights, or when Pops walked through the back door with his books and papers stumbling in before him. She'd crack a smirk that burst into a wide grin and then a blushing chuckle. I had kind of hoped there was going to be an addition, for her sake. It felt like she only lived for us.

But then Pop went to work one morning and never returned, and it's felt in every part of that house. Every dent in the walls where he'd bumped into it with one of his exciting work projects. The creek from every sudden swing of the doors, especially in the morning, and you'd hope to the light that rushes in that it was him.

"Where is he?

"Why did he leave?"

"And maybe.......with whom?"

The voices in my head were vibrating my metal ring off, banging my brain against this dentable metal it just keeps getting louder and louder....the more questions popped up, the louder it got... So much that before Mom got home, I went digging in his office/room for answers one day, and I found this note pad...I couldn't bring myself to go much further searching for what was written on it, until the other day...

That day I went to the public library... On the other side of town, to figure out what all these numbers could mean. I went that far because no one knew me there and I couldn't have Mom watching me or others from school annoying me. I wasn't sure if these were phone numbers, chemical equations or combinations to a safe somewhere. But I had to find out now!

I looked them over time and again so many times I've memorized them:

679. 887: 709. 227, 569N. 485SE: 237. 094

679. 887: 709. 227, 569N. 485SE: 237. 094...

679. 887: 709. 227, 569N. 485SE: 237. 094?

I sat there trying every combination, every number-driven source I could think of...I even tried channeling my father's essence, or at least how I saw him. The only thing I came back with was a huge headache. I was tapped on the hilt for all three closing updates...30mins...15mins...5... what library closes at 10 pm anyways!

"Ok, young lady you need to go now, we've closed 10mins ago!"

I didn't realize how late it had gotten. How much of a pain it would be to pass the donut shop on the way, and how upset Mom would get?

I think she overreacts sometimes, but looking back she reacted exactly as she should. As much as I knew this little fact, nothing but these numbers and what they could mean filled my mind. Before I knew it, I was stumbling through the back door at midnight, and mom was waiting by the counter. I didn't see the tears. I was in a daze. I only saw the steam coming off her face and I stood there for a blank minute then mumbled something she seemed to not have liked...

That slap woke me up, most definitely...

I thought it woke up the whole house and half the neighborhood. I knew Scribs was up...he's always sneaking around late at night, down to that basement of his. He is the only one that goes down there anyway, it's too creepy for anyone else it seems.

I was shaken to the blackness of my core... it hurt...it all hurts, I wanted to scream out...in pain, in frustration.

I missed my father. I missed the warmth of my mother...I miss what my family was...and I still don't know what these numbers are. I failed everyone and everything... And I'm just going to stay away from everybody...In my room and my mind.

Zombie mode...

Chapter 3H
Ninja style

So apparently, I created clones of myself...well a clone rather. It's not like the pencil that drew those stories in the Naruto Manga, he must be tired of seeing all the same lines over and over and over again and over again. I came straight home after school, I didn't want to get caught thinking and contorting my face. Everyone would know I'm lying about something... I had a lot on my mind after all.

I needed to get home before everyone else. But they must have read my thoughts, I had scribbled down all day in school because Jade and Mom beat me home and Ol' Yell...er wasn't far behind.

"Hi Moms, the Emerald Bubbler...how we doing today?" I said bracing for a quick tracing...But nothing from either side.

Things are still tense. No easy rubbing can erase that line drawn in the sand from the other night.

"Ok, if anyone needs me to referee, I'll be in my writing hole... Lots of homework to do."

I knew that they knew. I knew and I wanted to use the embarrassment and guilt of that to give me the space to think. I couldn't help thinking. I wanted to know... What was that...Where did that come from...could I do it again? What else could I do?

The disappearing thing and now I created a clone...another version of me...a doppelgänger!

All by the need and thought. My subconscious must have brought him to life while I was deep in my thought trance... Pacing back and front I didn't see him spring up from the paper and he must have been pacing in unison ever since. I just couldn't wrap my head around the process, but they say don't look a gift-wrapped cup of graphite tea in the...

Hold on...can I draw all the ice cream I want?...
How bout a graphite sandwich?...
Or some tape over Summer's mouth?
...That kid does nothing but scream...

I tried, over and over again, for what seemed like 2 hours.... But nothing but flat figures, all on paper...You know how much paper it takes to practice when you can't erase anything?

But I just kept doing them.

"Ahhh...nope, nope...

Nope…ahhh…

Nope… why? ….nope….

Now what is that?"

In the back of my mind I'm still thinking a couple of things: Why was the Mayor himself investigating a vandalism complaint? He's not a cop…and while he was talking he looked at me like he knew a lot more.

Where the heck is Berol? How was I going to get my book back? We most definitely saw rocket site, but what does it have to do with Pop and those numbers?

Chucked in these thoughts were some food-related ones…I thought a full stomach would help. Even better, a stomach filled with my favorite food….and I had tried to create them since…but I couldn't seem to do it? What's the point of having this ability when you can't do anything with it…whenever you want to. And now I've made myself ravenously hungry…. Let me run upstairs real quickly and grab something to munch on.

Up the stairs everyone was still sitting doing their various after school activities. Mom was cross hatching some test papers; at the other corner of the kitchen, Jade was penning some homework also there was the embarrassing tension line in the middle.

Dodo...do..do...Dodo...do...do...

Even Summer had a sense of fear to not try and wrestle attention her way. Piercing looks from mother to daughter were fired from one end to the next, but as quickly as the glance was fired it also missed. I saw that both wanted to apologize for more than just that night but it was too raw, too much to sort through, too many unanswered truths. And no one knew the questions to ask.

While I was doing the tango steps around it trying to grab a snack and get back to my questions...

"Door...Big Door..." - Summer murmured in between her airplane imitation and burbles.

No one looked up.

"Door!, Big Door...big Door..." She said more deliberately.

We all turned, expecting a tap, a knock a turn of the door handle even.

"Po..., I mean is someone there?"

There was no answer, but the shadow under the door stayed still for a second or two...

"Hello!?" - Mom said raising to push off from her chair, I knew she could make one big glide to get to the door, but I was quicker. as I opened the door... The shadow disappeared as quickly as if it was trapped by several spotlights on stage. Maybe it was a ninja giving into the darkness.

"No one was there...you scared them off with your face, Chumper."

"What did you say, boy?"

"Ahhhh...No one was there?"

"What?..."

"You're scary sometimes...you..." - I was cut off

"I told you not to call me Chumper."

This was a bad time to poke the bear, the nervous teenage dents in her face were starting to full out and heat the grooves of her joints as she loomed closer to me...She snatched me by my crown ring, which I quickly slid out of to get away. Yell was enjoying and envying the happenings, she started her chant...

"Bite...bite...bite....bite..."

It could have been "fight", but bite was more appropriate at the time...but she can't form her words properly, another disadvantage of a Mom that was too busy.

Mom went right back to her English Test papers series, ignoring who was at the door, the 3 ring circus in her kitchen, and more importantly what was left tucked in the right-hand corner away from where light hits right in the spine.

So it had concealed its form... Ninja style.

Chapter 4H

Look where you put your point

Berol put me in the spotlight when he stole my notebook from his father and dropped it by my house. He was careful not to be seen or followed, but that meant I couldn't be seen with this book...Ever.

Not at school or at home, I was not sure if the Mayor had gotten to the faculty about the "vandalizing logistic" caper as well as Berol's "behavior and influences". He dealt with this very vindictively, so I wasn't surprised that there was more probing phone calls to the house after that night. Mom was more irritable and defiant at home. So I couldn't be seen with Berol as much nor could I ignore him either. It was weird, but the next day, he was back at school. How was I going to play this?

"Hey Scribs...we should talk, but not here, of course, I'll meet you after school."

"Right..."

But before I turned around, he was halfway across the yard-, which in all honesty isn't hard since the surface of the school is on a more Bristol texture, that hardly leaves a graphite mark...perfect for easy cleaning. But still Berol sped away.

The school was easy today...I glided through the day with the quickness. I was not sure if it's the anticipation of after school or that I wasn't paying attention at all...But a loud bell shook me out of my academic slumber.

"Why am I just leaning against this wall, what is this strange pattern and what was that noise?"

"Well given that you are at school, and this is Visual Communication class, one would assume that those things would be considered hieroglyphs, demonic symbols, graffiti, tags of the vandalistic kind or simply art. I wasn't sure what they were so I've been erasing them...since...you can't!

"What did you say?" I spun around to see who this was...

"Calm down it's only me... your favorite neighborhood savior - Charc stated with her number 2 pushed up all proud. I expected stars and highlight lines to shoot out from behind her.

"You've been in a daze all art class, wondering from one end of the paper to the next, making those jerky twist and turns, jumps and sputters, but in that deliberate way only you can, which is when I realized you weren't yourself because you aren't that careless at school, especially when you know the consequences of the lock down. We know how much you hate being locked down...even though you love been in the basement the whole time. But cabin fever always comes up after 4 days... then you'd sneak over to my house... and....and..."

"Charc....Charc....Charc!" - I said,

"Thanks, but there is no need for the Charc Report right now!"

As much as I was grateful I couldn't allow her to run her mouth right now. I had a meeting that I had to make.

Chapter 5H
The meetings...

We were to meet outside the carving station...

He had this look on his face...one of all knowing and yet filled with ignorance. He keep saying," I knew it was you, I could see the three-sided deception, and the shakiness in your voice when you ran off earlier, that quick thinking reminded me of something...someone...

"You are supposed to be just stationery, a regular number 2 pencil, regulated to just one thought process, one way of being... Another tool in the pack, another stick in a cup. But I sensed the creativity, different shades... something odd, I won't call it special... Because I don't know what it is, but I know you've been hiding something boy."

Mayor Stanford was right there waiting for me. Stiff, looming and erect, He grinded his point into the ground. He had a sense of anger that I couldn't quite place...his mustache was almost on fire. Was it me, my existence, could he possibly know anything...everything? Was it Berol, was I the bad influence he didn't want spoiling his work?

Was it that he now had to take time off his busy schedule to play detective with some "deformed dull point"?

Grrrrr….

Either way, at this point,
I wasn't going to find out…not today…not right now so I
took off! Down the street, criss-crossing the side walks,
painted grass images, outlines of road ways…you name
it I was scuffing/marking/scratching it.
I didn't look back to see how far I had gotten, nor if I was
followed.

I was like a demon; like the game the children
used to play with us at their schools, where they'd hold
the top of your head pressing down as tight as possible,
then use their fingers I think the index and the thumb to
flick your point forwards, to see who had the longest line
mark.

I was doing that all over town, with longer quick streaking
marks. I just had to get away, my heart raced and as
my mind raced I was not sure where I was going…I just
needed to get away. Soon I paused to catch my breath
in the alley between "The Hollowed Point" donut shop
and the acrylic coating store "One Coat".

Finally, I looked around to see how far I got and
if I was followed. Although I knew he wouldn't follow;
he didn't look the type…So I doubled back to see him
just standing there…spinning…pacing. He looked rather
agitated than before…He seemed besides himself, and
he spoke loudly for everyone a few meters to hear…

I wanted to get closer, but I couldn't risk it...
I only heard every other word...

I didn't....to....want to do this...I didn't want anyone to know about....what.... those Pastelle are all the same!"

What was he saying...what did all of that mean...

"Betrayal, betrayal?" ...I didn't even know Berol was his son...Was the Mayor becoming unraveled by little ol' me? Why? Was he even talking about me?

He seemed way more agitated than he should be after he chased a lil' nub like me around...there must be more to the story...But I don't have time to be sitting in the bushes, pondering about someone that I left 5 minutes ago...I needed to get home.

And home I went...On through the weeds...wet grass...along the smooth sidewalk....just gliding away as fast as my little point could carry me.

My mind raced....my mind wondered, I figured that either Mr. Stanford would either deal with these agitations or finish me off at the source....my house...

Only my mother could help me now...but I had to get there first.

As I slid, something else started bothering me about Mr. Stanford's weird behavior...the way he kept rubbing the side of what should be his...temple. That's what humans call it, right?

It didn't feel weird...It felt somewhat....familiar and soothing; it was much like freshly ream paper with no imperfections and slightly warm...that I glided on like butter....that left a deep impression from the lightest touch.

I came out of my mind's rambling just in time to come up to my house. It was getting dark, I would be in trouble if Mom was there, but at this point, I didn't care as long as Mr. Stanford was not there and especially she hadn't got any whiff of this 'corrupting Berol business",

I wanted my mommy!!

The door creaked as it slowly opened...The light switches weren't on yet; we were just into twilight, so there was no slow illumination nor the boom of my mom's thunderous voice.... for now, the kitchen was clear.
I quickly took my crown off and stowed it away to rush to the basement...where I can do my best thinking and more importantly....hideout for a bit.

"Now where the heck have you been, bruv - Scribsy is it?"

"Berol, You sly devil!! - I shouted.

"You know your father is looking for you? How'd you even get down here? How long have you've been here? And how you didn't tell me anything about your father?"

And he just stared at me blankly as if I should already know all these answers. Why am I making him waste his breath?

"Scribs are you and Berol ok down there, sounds like you haven't been together for the last 2hrs...?" - The boom trailed off.

"So you've been here all this time, you didn't know about our would-be meeting downtown?"

I asked although I already knew the answer.

"Nope, and you're welcome...I covered your butt...again."

"You're welcome... I guess...Dude, your father looked off when I saw him at our meet up spot. I swore he was going to lock me up and torture me into leaving you alone, dude,"

"Well he did raise his voice at me saying to leave y'all alone when he found out I was hanging out around here. It's the first I've seen him visibly shaken, for 3 milliseconds as if he lost concentration."

"Yeah he's kind of intense like that...but I doubt he would go that far...He's no pen, his marks can be erased like the rest of us...."

"So what's going on with you...Berol?"

"Yeah my Father found the notebook you dropped, I had gone back and found it later that night. Some of the guards must have seen me lurking around at the rocket launch site...or someone saw me dragging my point back home late at night...Who knows?"

"My father apparently... - he continued

"He was pretty much waiting for me right in front of my room after I came in to check in on Mom and all. He thought we were out "plotting again" or something...he's always so serious. Now he seems to be watching and taking a much more keen interest in me of late...Some family legacy, first master pencils type stuff, I could count on Mom to block some of that stuff....But not anymore...I might be sent away to some "sharpening" school of the sort in back in England...I don't know bruv....It's a lot...

"What's with this Aquamarine stuff?" - I asked

I couldn't shake it...maybe with all this blue feeling going around...it made me think about the ebb and flow of the sea, calming things down, but still stressful when you look over the horizon and realize this whole big beautiful blanket of blues and greens.

"Oh, that...that's my mother's maiden name... so the kids wouldn't pick on me or I don't get special treatment from the teachers ploy" - he answered like a fat guy swatting away a fly.

I could see this whole thing with his father was stressing him out...it grinded his "rubber ring" into the soft developing wood of a young kid unsure of what was to become of his world up until now. The kid started to get

comfortable in his shiny acrylic skin, and now it's about to be shaved off for a new one given to him by his distant unrelenting father. It would stress out anyone, and this is the true meaning of stress.

So, I let him steam, chill, mark the floor up for a bit...get some of it out. But, most importantly, I thought to myself what were we going to do about my little issue with the Mayor? I just ran from him; he's sure to end up here eventually. I'd have nowhere else to run then.

Thankfully that day never came...and it never needed to, something much more devastating became more evident on a late Wednesday night weeks later...

Chapter 6H
Where am I, really?

Look out there...

The big blue ball in the dark sparkly sheet. Just like the human body, most of it is made of water, yet I wondered how they could abuse their environment so much. They looked for destructive energy when the vast bodies of water could sustain them for eons...like it had always done...naturally.

Yes, I often pondered...

How much measurement went into building the pyramids in Egypt or the wall of China or...hmmm. I can see all of them up here, on my perch.

It can get pretty dark up here...Here is my favorite crater... oh who am I? I'm lucky I guess...Lucky to witness all that I've seen...

But you can call me Slim, Slim Pastelle.

This is where I sit peering out to the world...literally. You see...Well, let's start from the top, I'm from a brand of pencils...the Pastelles.

My family...must be worried sick, they probably thought the worse...that I abandoned them. Dawn would probably track me down, chump, just like her mother would let me have it...But what I fear the most is the pain in little Scribs' eyes...

But this isn't of my doing, I've always taught my kids and openly spoke to anyone that would listen when I'm passionate...anyone that could hear: listen to everything, especially that little voice in your heart; you can be anything you want to be...following your dreams. My dreams were my thirst for knowledge, it led me to go to different places and I've met some pretty interesting people, and as much as going out into the world, they filled every inch of my heart & soul.

I think back to the day, Professor Bright came into the office just beaming and lost at the same time...

"I...I....I...I know what our next project is", pausing slightly.

"I know a place we could study that would give us a better understanding of ourselves and our place in this world...think of a place that's always been with us... it has guided us, but we've never spoken...it fills us with hope, wonderment and love...from far, far away."

His face lit up much like his name and the more he elaborated the more animated he got and everyone bought into the idea and the possibilities, even I could feel my ferrule tighten with anticipation, Can you imagine going to the moon?

With everyone on board, the team was now tasked with developing a means to study the moon. Prof. Bright wrote everything down, no idea was rejected initially, we were encouraged to just find a way... Over the years, this became known as the "Bright Flash"

Any thought complete or not, cryptic or simple, crazy or logical, used or revisited were jotted down. The team was encouraged to walk in teams, every human had their pencil teammate to catch every idea as soon as it happened.

Professor Bright tasked me with listing and making up the teams, which was four persons and a pencil. We intellectual types are more sociable than people give us credit, we don't all wear huge glasses and pocket protectors filled with pens. I don't even have a pocket. Plus, the company of pens can be tiresome, as they have a superiority complex-always going over my stuff when I was the one that came with the idea in the first place....Humph!

They grinded my point a bit...

So, months of collecting ideas ensued...

A giant slingshot, a tower, a huge gun with the traveler wrapped in rubber, a mechanical arm that flings an object up high like a catapult but with more velocity, a toaster like device, airplanes, replicas of a powerful bird, much like an eagle, missiles that don't explode (but how would we get it back down), a rocket ship? A spaceship? One we shot down in the Nevada desert, maybe?

Everything was written down in small notebooks, then transferred to the big idea book at the office, this was done to help tidy up and so that the thing was not forgotten or so it sparked an expansion of the idea. The time came...we were all called into the big conference room on the 5th floor. All my team was accounted for and ready and the humans were looking quite sharp as well, even Hoffman.

He was a stocky, sheepish looking man that was always biting on No.2.

No. 2 was my second in command. He's been here the longest, and he was a real trooper; he would always wrap himself with plastic tape so he looked all shiny and new again. He joked that it made him feel young, but we all know it was to stop good ol' nervous Hoffman from chewing on him. I asked him to team up with Hoffman, as he was the most experienced, and he could correct some written mistakes and jot down guide notes and words that would somewhat inspire his teammate.

We were in that conference room for what seemed for hours, going through every single idea in this huge leather bounded book. I'm sure it was custom made.

Now, I don't claim to know everything but, honestly, I mainly pay attention to things that affected me directly... There are many things I took for granted and downright disregarded. My head was so clouded with the pursuit and wonder of another world out there waiting to be discovered and all the knowledge it would take to get there that I lost sight of what was right in front of me...

I wandered around the dark side of the moon when I wanted to truly reflect on my thoughts. I liked to wander around in the dark; it matches parts of my mind that I try not to shine the light on.

I glided through the craters, but I was careful not to spend too much time in any of them since the craters are the point of impact for many flying rocks in outer space...I can't help but think that they are running away from something, something that eats metals, rocks and ice.

Anyways back to the light...

The main ideas that stuck out from the great custom made books were - if only for entertainment purposes the giant slingshot and coaxing a cow to train for the big jump over the moon and the spaceship which didn't exist, and the rocket.

Ultimately. Prof. Bright chose to go with a rocket.

Since no one on earth has ever built a rocket except for Hollywood, we got some engineers from other departments to join our little project. The engineers are the ones that made sure whatever we built didn't collapse or blow up.

I liked them. They are rulers and measuring tools and they have a funny little jig they do when they are quite pleased with themselves and they think no one's watching. I was the one that got to draw up the design for our little rocket ship, with a little help from SCRIBS, that boy was perfect for making stuff up, and with his instructions, we got the initial design for our own soon to be-spaceship.

After the engineers got it, we went through a little, friendly fight about what was or wasn't practical.

This was all on paper though. We imagined that the big fight would be when we finished and took the whole thing to the guys with the purse strings. But we didn't get much fight along the way in retrospect; I mean who wouldn't want to build a spaceship (engineers kept calling it a rocket or Transportation Propulsion Device, such Nerds!

The presentation day came...

"It's dark up in here..."

This reminds me of that morning....we were in the conference room in "perfect pitch darkness" *(as it was written down in the presentation notes, yes we prepare for everything...)*

And...

Wait, what am I doing...This isn't about me, you're my only company and I'm boring you with useless details...We got the green light and the money to build this rocket.

Thanks to the Mayor we found a secret and convenient dig site outside of my hometown. These were exciting times, even Ol' Stanford was there almost every day, at the time it didn't feel ominous, but we were far enough out of the town that our operation wouldn't affect the infrastructure of our blessed Gradetler or the next town over Pensvilletown... And we already donated to both towns to keep everything a secret and by extension every one safe. So, there was no need for him to be there to keep an eye on the investment.

But as I said it was exciting times so I understood... And build it we did!

A couple of prototypes, a few false starts and a couple of blow-ups. We had to readjust according to the nature of the massive momentum we were taking on, a collaborative project spanning 5 departments, 2 towns, and multiple tools...I was switched from the creative to the documentarian.

I wrote down everything I saw, heard and was told. Some might say I was a bit too thorough...But there was a limited amount of somes...
All my journaling involved facts and opinions that went to a small committee of the keen people and pencils.

I should have been more careful...not to be so slick, not to be so hard on the points, not to get caught up in this event and forget where I was and where I wasn't...

My appreciation for being in the cozy environment of Prof. Bright creatives, I didn't realize how privileged we were...to think out loud, dream out loud, draw on the walls, dig in with all our points and minds...

Now, I'm in a dark room I think, somewhere trying to keep my mind occupied to not go crazy...crazier? What time is it? I wish I was anywhere but here. And I don't even know where here is.

It's so dark...I'm not even sure if my eyes are open or closed...but let me continue to think or dream... sinking into this crater of the moon...where I should be... where my mind takes me.

Chapter 7H
The return...and another...

It's been 2weeks...2 whole point numbing weeks! Ever since I talked Berol down...and advised him to go back home, as it was more trouble than it's worth for him to run away right now, and since I would have to go with him, that he didn't want the Dawn Pastelle bloodhound on his trail for taking her favorite pencil.

Yeah...14 days and nothing.

No classes, no lunchtime point kicking, No "crown faking" make believe he's going to snatch the crown off my head showing everyone my obvious secret...No making fun of Charc and her fast-paced information-packed ramblings when she was asked one question or when she volunteered her cursive talk. No racing home from school, and secretly making sure I don't get messed up along the way.

He lived much further than I did... He stood taller than most kids, not just in size but in statue and valor, he was navy blue mixed with a brilliant black and gold lining his number 2 emblem on his forehead, it paled in comparison to the golden rings and that soft but stable eraser. Other people's rings were just gold in color, but his was something miners spent years looking for, a chip off ole Gibraltar, none of that shifting around a handful of dirt in river water, he was the real deal, his family line goes back to the old country so you'd expect as much. I couldn't do the same for him though, for most of his trouble was inside those big gates.

Yeah, No hellos, no calls, no nothing....

It was Pops all over again...We were planning to go check out the site again and find better clues for Pops' keeping everything else a secret except those numbers. We were to find out what made him so sloppy. Now Berol was missing too...I can't go through this again....I just can't. I shouldn't have to... But this time I had an idea. Well the source...Though it could mean a severe grounding and punishment from the Mayor, but how bad...?

Really, how bad could it be?

"Scribsy!"

"Yes, Mama...Do you need me? I'm trying to finish up some...eehm...homework..."

"Well, you need to eat honey. Your dinner has been getting cold, so come up so I can heat it up for you."

"I can do it. Remember you taught me...let me finish this first, you're the one telling us we should never leave things half done..."

"Ok, ok, ok smartallic…make sure you wash up…I taught you that too."

"Berol could be in trouble because of me…Berol could be in trouble because of me…Berol could be in trouble because of me."

I kept thinking over and over again. Did he snap? Did seeing his father, start him back up again? I should have let him live in our basement, or talk Mom into renting out half of my room - He could work it off… He's smart, and Mom and Summer love him…I don't know what Jade thinks of anyone anymore…she's still in zombie mood….

But what was I going to do…I had no best friend, and it's all my fault…it could be my fault…it might… something…maybe…. argh!! I really got himself into a tizzy again….the pacing, digging, marking, scraping, spinning….black marks all over the floor.

I glanced down….

"Shoot, Mom is going to kill me…….again," - I murmured

"You can say that again…."

"What? B? Where did you come…how did you?…"

"Yeah it's me.... well I'm not quite...I'm from you..."

"I drew you? When?"

"Just now...you didn't see...that was your intention at least."

"That was in the back of my mind...I was wishing you were here to help me through this..."

"Well, now I am... so, let's do this"

I hate talking to myself...kind of.

But for me...the other me was right. I needed answers. I needed to push past this and bring some sort of closure to fill the void Pops left... At least I should find out what happened.

It was another hour before we snuck out.

I had my dinner, and I didn't have to share...clones don't eat clay pizza. But we had to wait until everything slowed down a bit. Even though by the law of nature between kids, adults, and curfews it was the quietness that could have alerted every one of our leaving- two pencil points slowly gliding out the back door is bound to squeak.

Passing through the town this time was easier and quicker than the last, because I knew where I was going and where to avoid entirely. It was dark in the Mayor's office- less 'pitch blacky' and more the 'I wish it didn't exist' type of black.

The observatory fence was fortified. A second fence was erected with a 3feet gap between them both and razor wire on top...spiraling well in control and perfect alignment to keep us out.

"Where's the back door? These secret lairs always had one or two conveniently placed somewhere...or is it not that type of story?" - I said in huffrustration as we paced about 5mins looking for some break or weakness in the fence.

"Why don't you just draw us an entrance?" The fake Berol said.

"Do what?"

"Draw an entrance, a door, a ramp...something... but we can't just be standing out here dodging spotlights." - Berol two said louder.

"Listen, I still don't fully understand how you're here..., so explain to me how this magic thing work."

"Well…ahhh…first you…then you…after that… hmmm…"

"Yeah, The last doppelgänger couldn't tell me either…"

"I was going to tell you in the best way possible, but you interrupted…
You seem to be able to create things as you really need them and we need to get into that facility right now…so the simplest way is to concentrate on the finished result, with me you used Berol as a subconscious inspiration or reference, so focus on getting us in and let your subconscious figure it out, we don't have the time to be developing lesson plans on creating "magic" as you put it…"

I ran my point along the edge of the fence…trying my best not to touch it…thinking a running start and big push should get us over there…or a rocket backpack… or a mini helicopter…or a trampoline…

Pacing up and down…. thinking…focusing…
I heard the steel wheel clicking, than a slow compression….
I turned around to see Berol two opening a metal trapdoor and beckoning me over to come on down…

"You did it!".

We followed a complete set of metal ladder rungs

down the scarcely lit hole…perfectly cut as if it was supposed to be there, but it disappeared as soon as we descended. We dropped down and hid behind the first and largest filling cabinet we saw. We peeked around to see pencils or people around. Then we delved deeper into a larger tunnel base of operation that had vents, decontamination areas, glassed secured rooms, large metal doors with no hinges, key panels and closets… with the same types of jumpsuits hanging in them…not sure of the color though, but they were bright, especially when the overhead lights hit them.

If I was on a school trip, I'd be more fascinated, but there was this uneasiness in the air filling up the huge ceiling less space. We snuck in the observatory and the deeper we went the larger it became…this didn't look like somewhere my Pop would abandon his family to hang out in every day, so he had to be locked in here somewhere, or maybe he was being experimented on…Or maybe he's just lost…Pops can be wispy and times. Whatever the reason my father found it interesting enough to write down coordinates in his notes over and over again, sort of like a school girl obsessed with her first crush.

"Hey remember we are supposed to be hiding…" Berol two mockingly reminded me as I was too busy looking all around in awe.

"But remember we don't know what we are looking for…not really" - I sheepishly shot back.

"So, we are on a we will know when we see it type of trip? …Then what about him…we know him right?"

There he was… the missing Mayor Stanford, standing on the platform, surveying it like a king surveys his kingdom and all the adoring peasants. He stood there for a long time looking or waiting on something. But this wasn't even his town. Why was he here with that much confidence?…Why?

We watched him for 5mins, partly trying not to be seen and partly planning our next move… But then someone approached…

"Mayor Stanford, what brings you to our facilities today, you don't trust we know what we are doing?"

A real stern rigid pencil that had to be in the military walked up…. He was what mom would call a real "stick in the mud", and he was the firm distraction we needed to move. Although we didn't know where we were going to, we knew that it had to be out of sight. We glided to what we thought was the back of this larger place; we slipped through this small door that was ajar, which was weird since everything else was locked down tight. And as this suspicion dawned on us the door suddenly closed behind us. We couldn't see the air in front of our face. But we were freezing. Were we locked in a freezer? We wandered around for a while not touching anything and jotting along like a dotted line. The only source of light was behind us from the locked door; then an opening came out of nowhere, but we were in very low light, and it's the only way forward…This would be a tight squeeze for a normal size pencil, but perfect for us. Great.

But then we realized the angle of darkness we were hoping for wasn't ideal…So as it reluctantly gulped us down further into itself, we stumbled over edges, but we grabbed the wall to balance ourselves, to break our fall and to act as a guide. We felt the coldness of the smooth concrete foundation, then it changed into bumps and lines of brick and mortar, definitely not new bricks, these had chips -wear and tear- to them. The farther down we went the cooler it got, and the more natural the air felt. I felt as if I was being drawn to somewhere, something…a destiny…a purpose, but right now I'd settle for getting away and staying safe and sound.

"Where the heck is this place? It felt like we found the prison, are we even still in the facility?" - murmured Berol two

"Something does feel different about this place, if you wanted to hide something, this would be the place alright."

"It's so dark in here. Wait, I can hear murmuring… mumbling rather…is that someone talking to themself? Do you hear that?" - Berol two said

The voice was eerie and low….a soft vibration as the words hit the floor, then rose to mix with the darkness of the air…disappearing or hiding in it and just making its presence known in the ear…like a soft explosion on the drums…

"Ye…ye…Yeah…" - I dragged myself forward
I was just afraid that it might be a ghost…I was afraid I knew that ghost…

"Where's that tune from…who would be singing in a place like this…?"

"Could this be the song of the dead?"

"Over the moon glow…all points to the sky… write your blessings in…pick a cluster of stars…look as the cattle rises…." The voice sang.

"Quite odd for a ghost to be singing show tunes, but I don't know that one…" - Berol two turned to me … He was about to continue but I stopped him…

"I know that song…I know that tune…it's not a show tune…it's a nursery rhyme…

…as the animals howl…all utensils cackle…to the sound of the fiddling diddle all the way till noon……" - I hummed aloud in reply

Yup….That's my Pops!!

Chapter 8H
Yeah...HOW DID I GET HERE anyways...

From the flickering of three bars of light...I could finally see clearly...

"Pops...Pops.... Are you ok...Pops?"

"Scribs...I..I..is that you ...No it couldn't be... How'd you get all this way on this side of the moon?... Where's your mooo..."

He trailed off, still in a daze from isolation and tethering on the brink of sanity. After seeing him like... like...this imagined, scenarios involving fire, drawing black holes and the complete eradication of all their future and past existence for all responsible, persons, pencil or percils...whatever or whomever was responsible.

It took a moment and basked in my anger, we finally picked him up; He was extra leaky and weak as if he'd been soaking in hot water for 5 days. Heavy was the father we had to lug around.

"We have to get him out of here..." - Berol two chimed in.

"Yeah...but how? We don't know where we are or how we even got in here much less."

"Well, the most logical way is to either move forward and see what's ahead of us or go back from where we came and see how we could get that door open...We didn't try we just scampered off, like scared little kids "

"All truths... Pops is of no help right now. Let's go back...it might end up being shorter"

Shuffling back into the darkness the smell was pungent, sharp and overwhelming...An oppression had filled the room, but we stumbled on aware but with more determination than desperation. We leaned Pops against the wall near the door and we ran our search along the edges, up and down back and forth, pulling and jiggling the door handle, giving the door the biggest yank possible, but only receiving an slight defiance after it solidly did not-budge. If the door was in England, it would be guarding Buckingham Palace right now. We needed another way through this door...a key, a pick... even prying off the edges something....After fumbling in the dark, a few candidates came up...some lint, a plain of glass and a thread of metal...so really one...

"It's turning something...I almost...got something...right about...."

But wiggling the metal into the keyhole ...that proved...

"That w...w.. won't work either... I tried, probably with that same piece of wire too..." - Pops murmured.

"Mr. Pastelle...don't try and talk...we have to try something...and we are ways out...you're going to need your strength for when Ol' Scribsy Whisby thinks of something to draw us out..."

"I'm sorry....I tried...rubbed my point down to a stub trying to dig and claw my way out of here...I haven't seen any other way; let's go back to the moon and watch over your sisters and mother..."

"Yeah, Pops...I will get you out of here and get you home...we all need you... and you do not call me that!"

"How did you get in here anyway......" - and he trailed off again.

"Yeah...HOW DID YOU GET DOWN HERE??"

This booming voice filled with anger and shock... rushed into the room as fast as the door was flung open. I jumped back moving so the door wouldn't crush me or Pops,. Thankfully, the clone quickly disappeared; he must have slid to the back of the room. I could hear the squeaking of a fast moving sharp point, by then.

Mayor Stanford lunged at me, but I rolled under the nearest table…he tried his best to grab me, but every time he'd go right. I'd go left…then right…left…up then down …until his anger soared and he flipped the table over…so hard it flew to the other side of the room with a clan-clickity-clang…wiggly-wiggle…pan. I spun around rubbing all the paint off my backside to get away and he grabbed on to my crown and it ripped off with a loud long tear…

He was like a magician pulling out reams of handkerchiefs…pulling and pulling and I kept spinning… my crown was being ripped to shreds.. All the while he talked down to me as I glanced over to my barely conscious father…Help me, Dad.

"I knew it was YOU…only the son of this uppity, simpleton, black smudger, dreamer that wishes he could shoot color out of his number 2 point, could cause me so much stress…"

"I bet he set this all up unwittingly…as usual… good ol' Lucky Pastelley. We used to call him lucky because he could be unprepared for a test in school… hell…even life and everything would work out in his favor, and he didn't even want much….just Dawny. As sweet as she was even back then…I could see there was more to have…but you…You…YOU!!"

I laid there woozy and somehow wrapped up into the rings of my makeshift crown. It doesn't look as if I'm going to get Pops or myself out of here after all...I could see and feel him as he glided menacingly over to where Pops was...He bounded him while he mockingly mumbled at him...

Like a predictable villain, he was monologuing...

"You didn't want to lend me your luck...your skill... you wanted to take the moral high ground. Stealing is wrong, even if it's from ones that took advantage of your kindness and didn't understand that a single difference doesn't make you a monster or a weirdo...Numby... Numby I hated that name...Kids are cruel, but when validated by adults...that hurt even more. I just wanted someone to understand and someone to pay, feel my pain or similar. And they sure did...But that didn't last long because you didn't show up and I got caught halfway down the road, I broke that glass sharpener into a million pieces though...I needed your luck Slim...I needed you..."

"Ahhh....ohhhh..." Pops just whimpered

"The drugs are taking effect again...just stay here a while, let me get your son to join you in your cell just as loopy as you..."

He was coming back towards me with a sad yet sadistic hurtfulness in his eyes…which disappeared the closer he got to me. He took a shiny syringe with a large sturdy needle…my eyes widen and my brain began to boil…the thoughts all start racing to the front. Someone yelled fire and flood and locust in my head, and they all had to get out at the same time…The closer he got the more they pushed…

"Turn into a jellyfish… No, a giant octopus, wrap your tentacles around him and toss him to the back of the facility that we didn't want to go into earlier…no… turn into a bear…we are on land!"

He was right on top of me now, and he was blocking the brilliant flash of light that had rushed into the room…someone was coming and he had to move fast…So I had to move even faster.

"Why not draw a huge punching glove to knock him on his ass"…as he brought the needle down, I stuck my point to the ground then flicked it up like a striking match and swoosh, poof a huge white puffy light came out between us and flung Mr. Stanford across the room, and I was free. Moving towards where Pops was….

"T…Tori…Victor is that you, where have to been all this time??" - Pops said…standing up now…he leaned against the wall.

I had trouble explaining to myself what happened, the flash, the shockwave, the push, …the needle. I tried to go over everything with Pops while processing it in my head also (I have to learn to control these skills or whatever you want to call them), but he was more concern with Mr. Stanford, who's point was up in the air and also on the ground…?

"Tori what have to done…what have you done to yourself?"

He stood up and he had a crown that was freshly broken off. This was much more sophisticated than mine but that wasn't the shocker…His points, he was sharpened at both ends.

"Slim…don't ever call us that ever again…we are not kids anymore…and we are not friends."

"Hey, psst…when you're done staring at that ol' pencil case over there…you might want to get out of here real fast…we're about to have some loud and angry company….I gave them the slip earlier but I am sure they followed me back here" - Berol two tapped me on the shoulder and whispered.

By then all the lights were flung on…especially the bright red flashing ones and the faint white lights from before became steady, forceful and plentiful, the Calvary was here! Except we weren't supposed to be here…Especially crown-less me.

Mr. Stanford was standing near the door, so they grabbed him first, they were too shocked to see him like that they paused just staring, but that soon faded and he was yanked through the door...the multiple voices and tones...shouting, gasping and carrying-on.

"What are you, have you gone mad Mr. Mayor?"

"Grab him...don't let him escape..."

While all of this was happening father had become more lucid. Maybe it was the shock of what he just saw: what he thought was a ghost from the past, or maybe the urgency that he has been locked down here for how long and looking to get out, or maybe he realized that his son was down here and there are armed guards on their way back into "sweep"...I grabbed his hand and we bolted towards where Pops was being kept. Neither of us knew what to do beyond that point, but we didn't care...fresh air was coming from that direction Berol two lead the way, so there was hope.

I'm not sure how things worked out but it did...
A paved pathway showed up with some nicely drawn arrows "this way out" on the wall, it got brighter the farther we went, and they collapsed right after we passed. Pretty soon we were way out of the range of the coordinates and farther away from the observatory secret base. We came out at the meadow right in the middle of Gradetler.

"We're almost home Pops…just a little farther…"
- I whispered

We made it a couple more steps, out spinning around to take in our surrounding…

"Scribble, my boy" - giving me one of the biggest tightest bestest hugs…

"Where are we…You wouldn't believe the dream I've been having…You wouldn't…I…I get to dream about my boy…my special boy…I knew there's something in him waiting to come out, bright for us to see…Go share it with the world Scribs, I know you can do anything you put your mind to…You were born with a gift, you don't need an eraser to keep practicing…pay attention and make it perfect… I know you will……..Snorezzzzz"

I'm not sure if was the adrenaline fading or the fresh air sped up into our faces or with all his journeys and fights and drugs, But he fell into a peace-filled sleep.

Chapter 9H
Dethroned prince

I was crown-less…in the middle of town… with a passed out father on the grass, not many people know me like this and I'd rather keep it that way, for now. …I had to get home or at least out of sight but my passed out father would only slow me down.

I didn't know where the real Berol was, and I don't think Charc could ever keep this much of a secret for 5 seconds, and I can't conjure clones and disappearing acts right now…I still haven't fully figured that out yet.

Oh Oh…I know…I know I can call home…Jade should be home, let's use her zombie-ness to our advantage and cure it at the same time.

"Woohooo!!, I mean H…H…ello…" - in my best grifter voice.

"…Yes…who is this…Mom is not home right now…But I'll give her the message…You do have a message right…" she said hurriedly,-in her best can't be bothered voice.

"Yes…Write this down…. 6 7 9. 8 8 7: 7 0 9. 2 2 7, 5 6 9 N. 4 8 5 S E: 2 3 7. 0 9 4"

"Wait who is this, is this some sort of sick game?"

"Do you want to see your father again or not? Come to the playground in the middle of town right before the Razor's Edge barbers…" - and I hung up faster than flipper could.

I made sure Pops was secure. No strange termites lurked around and I bolted to the back of a line of houses where the grass was at it's highest, ducked and rolled, flicked and skipped down like the smoothest paper ever pressed…I also moved parallel to the street so I could get a glimpse of Jade tearing up the streets to check out this mysterious call. You should have seen her…She was moving with purpose and speed for someone of her size.

I slipped into the kitchen door, Mom and Yell had just come in maybe minutes before and plopped down in the couch seemingly exhausted…I slid down to the basement and waited…all the while wondering…

What was going to happen to Mr. Stanford? I don't fully understand my "gifts", but can I now control them?, How many clones can I make?

Pops seemed to be friends with Victor "Tori" Stanford when they were younger… Does Mom know him? Does she remember? Will Pops remember?

I don't want to end up like that...he used to be me...I understood some of what he was saying...I need someone to keep me grounded...Where's my anchor... Where's my best friend...What happened to Berol?

I heard a loud thud as the door was flung open... Screams and screams...

The loud boom that followed jolted me and like a light bulb exploding above my head, I immediately reached out to grab the top of my head...

Oh no, I forgot the crown!

"SCRIBS!!!, Where did this come from?"

Jade asked while as she stomped down the stairs...

"Come see what I found in the bushes..."

A 41-year-old Jamaican Graphic Designer, Illustrator with interest in many things including the environment and human behavior. Making my debut in writing, paying homage to the second most important tool in the world next to the creative mind (in my opinion).. the pencil!

A wonderful tool that has been in my life and others for more than 4 decades. you see it in my illustrations over the years, giving products and ideas life.

Forever punctuating my words and scribbles...

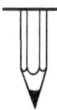

for more info check www.scribblespencil.com

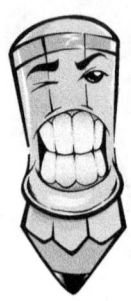

Coming Soon

IN THE SERIES OF PENCIL JOTTINGS;

-The New Dawn and other cursive points.

- A Colorful Summer.

Copyright © 2020 by André Hutchinson

All rights reserved. No part of this book may be reproduced or
transmitted in any form or by any means without written permission
from the author.

www.ingramcontent.com/pod-product-compliance
Lightning Source LLC
Chambersburg PA
CBHW070041030726
47506CB00003B/822